H. M. Ranga

The Adventure of
the Secret Necklace

D1643125

The Adventure of the Secret Necklace

Enid Blyton
Pictures by Mark Robertson

Bloomsbury

The publishers would like to thank David Barnhouse, Kelly Slocombe and Jon Tolley of Hugh Sexey School, Blackford, Wedmore, Somerset for their enthusiasm and participation in the photographic shoot for this cover. Photograph taken at Yew Tree House, Blackford, Somerset

All rights reserved; no part of this publication may be reproduced or transmitted by any means, electronic, mechanical, photocopying or otherwise, without the prior permission of the publisher

The Adventure of the Secret Necklace was first published by
Lutterworth Press 1954
First Published by Bloomsbury Publishing Plc in 1997
38 Soho Square, London W1V 5DF

Enid Blyton

Copyright © Text Enid Blyton Limited 1954
Copyright © Illustrations Mark Robertson 1997
Copyright © Cover photograph Katie Vandyck 1997

The moral right of the author and illustrator has been asserted
A CIP catalogue record of this book is available from the
British Library

ISBN 0 7475 3211 7

Printed in Great Britain by Clays Ltd, St Ives plc

10 9 8 7 6 5 4 3 2 1

Cover design by Mandy Sherliker

CONTENTS

CHAPTER 1

AN EXCITING LETTER

'Ding-ding-ding-a-ding!' A bell jingled loudly downstairs, and there was a scurry and a yell from upstairs.

'Bob! There's the breakfast bell! Can you do my dress up at the back for me? Quick!'

Bob went to his twin sister, Mary. 'Why do girls have dresses that do up at the back?' he grumbled. 'I hate all these hooks and things.'

'There are only two,' said Mary. 'Hurry, Bob, we'll be late!'

Bob hurried, and the hooks went into the eyes neatly. Then both children raced downstairs and into the breakfast-room. Daddy was just about to sit down.

'Ha! It's you, is it?' he said. 'I had a feeling it was an elephant or two crashing down the stairs. You're just in time.'

The twins kissed their mother and father and

sat down to their breakfast. Mary's sharp eyes caught sight of a letter on her mother's plate.

'You've got a letter,' she said, 'and I know who it's from. It's from Granny! I always know her big, spidery writing. Open it, Mummy. Perhaps she is coming to stay with us.'

Mummy opened the letter and read it. 'No – she's not coming to stay,' she said. 'But she wants *you* to go! Would you like to?'

'Oh *yes*!' said both twins together. They had only once been to stay with Granny, when they were very tiny, because she lived rather a long way away – but they remembered her old, old house with its strange corners and windows.

'When can we go?' asked Bob. 'As soon as we break up school? I'd like to see Granny again. She's strict, isn't she – but she's kind too. I like her.'

'I *love* her,' said Mary. 'I love her twinkly eyes, and her pretty white hair – and I don't mind her being strict a bit, so long as I know what she's strict about. I mean, she tells us what she doesn't like us to do, so we *know*. Can we go soon?'

'Granny says as soon as school ends, you may go to her,' said Mummy, reading the letter again. 'And one of the reasons she wants you is that she will have another child staying there – and she thinks it would be very nice for him to have your company – somebody to play with.'

'Oh,' said Bob, not quite so pleased. 'I thought we would be having Granny to ourselves. Who's the other boy?'

'Your cousin Ralph – you've never seen him,' said Mummy. 'Your granny is *his* granny too, because his daddy is brother to your daddy, and Granny is their mother.'

The twins worked this out. 'Oh yes,' said Mary. 'We've never seen Ralph. Why haven't we?'

'Only because your uncle John, his daddy, has had to travel about all over the place, taking his wife and child with him,' said Daddy, looking up from his paper. 'Very bad for the boy – no proper schooling, no proper home. You two will be good for him.'

The twins didn't feel as if they wanted to be 'good for him'. It made them sound like medicine or stewed apples or prunes – things that were always 'good for you'.

'How old is Ralph?' asked Bob, hoping he wouldn't be much older than he was.

'Let me see – you're seven – and Ralph is almost a year older – he'll be about eight,' said Mummy. 'I've no idea what he's like, because your uncle and aunt have been out of the country for two years now, and they never send any photographs. I expect he will enjoy having two cousins to play with.'

The twins got on with their breakfast. They weren't quite sure about Ralph – but when they began to think about Granny, and her old house, and the big garden with its fruit trees and flowers, they smiled secretly at one another.

'Lovely!' thought Mary. 'It's fun to go and stay in a new place.'

'Fine!' thought Bob. 'I wonder if that little pony is still at Granny's – we were too little to ride him last time – but this time we could. And I hope Jiminy the dog is still there. I liked old Jiminy.'

There was only one more week of school to go. When the last day came, the twins raced home. 'Mummy! Where are you? We've got some good news!'

'What is it?' said Mummy, looking up from her mending.

'We're top of our class – *both* top together, Bob and I!' shouted Mary. 'Isn't that a surprise?'

'Well, you've worked hard,' said Mummy, simply delighted. 'I really *am* proud of you. Dear me, to think I am one of the lucky mothers whose children work hard enough to be top!'

Daddy was pleased too. 'I shall give you each five pounds,' he said. 'You can take it to spend when you are away at Granny's.'

Five pounds! What a lot of money that seemed! Bob and Mary at once thought of ice-creams by the dozen, bars of chocolate, toffees and books and new crayons.

'Only two days more and we go to Granny's,' said Bob, putting his money carefully into a little leather purse. 'We're lucky – top of our form – five pounds each – and a lovely holiday at Granny's!'

Only two days more – and away they would go!

CHAPTER 2

ALL THE WAY
TO GRANNY'S

The twins helped their mother to pack their clothes in a small trunk. 'It's a good thing it's summer-time,' said Mummy. 'Your things take up so little room when they are just cotton frocks and shorts and shirts.'

'Don't put in any jerseys and mackintoshes,' begged Mary. 'We shan't need those!'

Mummy laughed. 'What a thing to say! What would Granny think of me if the weather turned cold or wet, and you hadn't a single jersey or mackintosh to wear? Don't be silly, Mary!'

Bob knew why Mary had said that. The weather was so lovely just then, the sky so blue, the sun so hot that it seemed quite impossible to think of cold or rain.

'Holiday weather!' he said. 'You won't miss us *too* much, will you, Mummy?'

'Not if you are happy and having a good

time,' said Mummy. 'I'll be glad for you, you see. It will be strange without you, of course – but Granny's sweet and kind, and she will look after you well for me. Now – where did I put those sandals?'

'Here they are,' said Bob. 'Have we got to keep very very *clean* at Granny's, Mummy? Cleaner than at home?'

'Well, Granny has always said that your daddy was just about the dirtiest little boy she ever knew,' said Mummy, smiling. 'So I don't expect she'll mind if you do get a bit dirty sometimes.'

'Goodness, was Daddy *really* a dirty little boy?' said Mary, in astonishment, thinking of her big, clean, nice-smelling father, with his polished shoes and well-scrubbed hands. 'Bob – maybe one day you'll be as clean as Daddy!'

'There – that's really everything, I think,' said Mummy, shutting down the lid. 'Now, what's the time? We've got just half-an-hour to label the trunk and strap it up safely, and get you ready. I'm going to take you and your luggage to the station in the car.'

The twins got themselves ready, and then went to say goodbye to their playroom and all the things in it. Mummy had packed Bob's monkey, which he couldn't bear to leave behind, and Mary's third-best doll, Elizabeth.

'Although she's only my third-best, I love her

most of all,' Mary said. 'She's cuddly, and she's got a nice smile, and she goes to sleep beautifully. Please pack her *very* carefully, Mummy.'

At last they were on the way to the station. The porter came to get their trunk. Mummy bought the tickets and there they were, standing on the platform waiting for the train to rumble loudly into the station.

It came at last, whistling shrilly, making Mary jump. Mummy put them into a carriage. 'I'll tell the guard to come and have a look at you now and then,' she said. 'You'll be quite all right, because you don't have to change anywhere. Eat your sandwiches when you see a clock on some station pointing to half-past twelve.'

'Goodbye, Mummy!' cried both children, hugging their mother and feeling suddenly that they didn't want to leave her behind. 'We'll write to you.'

'Bob, you'll remember that brothers *always* have to take care of their sisters, won't you?' said Mummy, 'So look after Mary. Goodbye, dears, have a lovely time!'

The guard whistled and waved his green flag. The train grunted and went off again, pulling the carriages in a rumbling row. The twins leaned out of the window and waved wildly. When at last they could see the platform no longer they sat back in the carriage.

'It's awfully grown-up, going on a long journey by ourselves like this,' said Mary. 'I hope half-past twelve won't be a long time coming. I feel hungry already.'

'Goodness! It's not half-past ten yet,' said Bob. 'You can have some chocolate at eleven. Mummy gave us a bar each. What shall we do now? Look out of the window – or read our books?'

'Oh, look out of the window!' said Mary. 'Let's have half-an-hour at that, then eat our chocolate, then have a game of seeing who can count the most houses out of the window. Then we'll watch for a station clock to tell us if it's lunch-time.

The time flew by. Soon they were having their lunch, and how hungry they were. Mummy had packed up some sardine sandwiches, tomato sandwiches, big pieces of fruit cake, a banana each, and another two bars of chocolate. They ate every single thing.

The guard came along every now and again and chatted to them. He said he would be sure to tell them when they arrived at the right station.

'We'll know all right,' said Bob, rather grandly. 'We'll be looking out ourselves.'

But, you know, they weren't! They both fell fast asleep after their lunch, and didn't wake up till the guard came along, shouting 'Curlington Junction! Curlington!'

He put his head in at their window. 'Hey! You there! Wake up, and get out quickly! I've got a porter for your luggage, and he's taking the trunk out of my van.'

Goodness! The twins almost fell out of the carriage in their hurry – and there, not far away, standing on the platform anxiously looking for them, was Granny!

She saw them at once and ran to them, hugging them both at once.

'Bob! Mary! Here you are at last, darlings! I've been so looking forward to seeing you. Come along – I've got the pony-trap outside, waiting. We'll soon be home.'

Out of the station they went – and there, in the little cart, was the pony they used to know. What a lovely beginning to a holiday!

CHAPTER 3

COUSIN RALPH

The porter brought out the small trunk that the children had with them, and stowed it in the pony-cart. Bob and Mary went to pet the small chestnut pony.

'Hello, Bonny! Do you remember us?' asked Bob. 'You're fatter, Bonny! Mary, he remembers us!'

'Of course he does,' said Granny, getting into the little pony-cart and sitting down. 'He hopes you are old enough to have a ride on him this time. Ralph rides him quite a lot.'

'Where *is* Ralph?' asked Mary, climbing into the little cart too. 'Why didn't he come with you to meet us, Granny?'

'I told him to,' said Granny, 'but when I was ready to start he was nowhere to be seen. He's probably stalking Red Indians or looking for spies, or ambushing bandits.'

'Oh,' said Mary. This sounded rather good. The twins liked playing at Red Indians themselves!

'Is Ralph nice?' Mary asked Granny.

'Well, now, I wouldn't tell you he wasn't, would I?' said Granny, cracking her whip a little to make Bonny go a little faster. 'You wait and see. You're all my grandchildren, and I'm fond of every one of you. Get up, there, Bonny, you're very slow today! Surely you don't mind two or three in the cart and a small trunk!'

Bonny trotted on, flinging his head into the air every now and again. His little hooves made a merry clip-clopping noise. The children felt very happy.

'I do like the beginnings of things,' said Mary, suddenly. 'The beginnings of a holiday – the beginnings of a pantomime – the beginnings of a picnic. I wish beginnings lasted longer.'

'They'd be middles then!' said Bob. 'Granny, will it be tea-time when we get home with you? I feel as if it might be.'

Granny laughed. 'Oh yes, it will be tea-time – with new bread and my own strawberry jam – and honey from my own bees – and a chocolate sponge cake made by Cookie – you remember her, don't you? And some of those chocolate biscuits you like so much.'

'Oh! Fancy your remembering that we like chocolate biscuits!' said Mary, pleased. 'You really are a proper granny.'

That made Granny laugh again. 'Oh, I'm a proper granny all right, so just mind your P's and Q's!' she said, with a twinkle in her eye. 'Now – here we are. Welcome to Tall Chimneys!'

That was the strange name of Granny's old house, and it suited it very well, because its chimneys were very tall indeed – old, old chimneys made of red brick like the house itself.

'I like your house, Granny,' said Mary. 'It looks old and friendly and – well, rather mysterious too. As if it had quite a lot of secrets.'

'It probably has,' said Granny, getting down. 'It's a few hundred years old, you know. Now, here comes Mr Turner to take the trunk. We'll go in.'

'Hello, Mr Turner!' called Bob. 'I remember you! And oh – here's Jiminy! Jiminy, do you remember us?'

A black spaniel ran up to them, barking a welcome. The children fell on him at once. 'Jiminy! You're just the same – but *you're* a bit fatter too! Your tongue's just as licky. Granny, he's licked my face all over.'

'Then I suppose you won't think it needs washing, but it does!' said Granny. 'Take the trunk up to the corner bedroom, Mr Turner, and then take Bonny to the stables. I shan't want him any more today.'

Turner, big and strong, lifted the trunk as if it were nothing but a box of chocolates, and ran up the stairs with it. The children went indoors, with Jiminy leaping round them in delight.

'Do you know the way up to your room?' asked Granny. 'You remember? Very well, go up now, and just wash your faces and hands. You'll find a comb there for your hair.'

The twins ran up the big, curving staircase. They remembered the little corner bedroom, with its slanting ceiling – lovely!

'Here it is,' said Bob, running in. Then he stopped suddenly. A loud fierce voice sounded from somewhere nearby.

'Spies! I know you! Put your hands up or I'll shoot!'

There was a loud *bang* as if a shot had gone off. Mary gave a scream and clung to Bob. Then the door of a cupboard was flung open and out stalked a big boy, dressed in cowboy things. He grinned at them.

'Did I scare you? I hope I did! I'm Ralph!'

The twins stared at him. 'What was that bang?' said Mary, her heart still beating fast.

'A paper bag! I blew it up and popped it to make you think it was a shot!' said Ralph, grinning. 'I'm glad you've come. It's awfully dull here. You look rather small, though – only just little kids. That's a pity.'

'We're seven,' said Bob, 'so we're *not* little kids. You're not much older yourself, anyway.'

'I'm bigger, though – much bigger,' said Ralph. And indeed he was. He grinned and stamped out of the room. The twins looked at each other.

Were they going to like him – or weren't they? They felt very doubtful indeed!

CHAPTER 4

AT GRANNY'S

The twins washed their hands and went down to tea. As Granny had said, it was a very fine tea. Bob and Mary sat down, looking at the well-spread table in delight.

Ralph came in, and sat down too. He smiled cheekily at his grandmother. 'I'm sorry I wasn't about when you went,' he said. 'I forgot the time.'

'I didn't really expect you,' said Granny. 'Will you please go and wash your hands and face, Ralph, and take your cowboy hat off? I've told you that before.'

'I'll just take my hat off,' said Ralph, and threw it on the floor. Then he reached out for the bread-and-butter.

'You heard what I said, Ralph,' said Granny. 'No tea unless you come properly washed and tidied. Don't let me have to find fault with you in the first few minutes your cousins are here!'

Ralph scowled. He gave the table leg a kick, got up and went out of the room. He certainly didn't like being scolded in front of his small cousins!

'Ralph is very big for his age, isn't he?' said Mary, making herself a fine strawberry jam sandwich. 'This *is* lovely jam, Granny – just as nice as Mummy makes at home.'

'That's good,' said Granny. 'Yes, Ralph *is* big for his age – but I expect you'll find that you know much more than he does. You can teach him a lot.'

This sounded rather surprising to Bob and Mary. 'Can't he read then – or do sums?' she asked.

'He only reads comics, not books,' said Granny, 'and that's a pity. He's not *very* good at sums, either – but that's not quite what I meant. Anyway, you'll soon find out. He's a good boy at heart and I'm very fond of him. He'll soon shake down and be sensible, now you've come.'

Mary hoped that he would! She hadn't forgotten the fright she had had when he had yelled from the cupboard, burst the paper bag, and flung himself out suddenly into their bedroom.

Ralph came down looking clean and cheerful. He made a simply enormous tea, and had to go out and ask for more bread-and-butter and honey.

'You'll have to grow more corn for bread, keep more cows for butter, and more bees to make honey, if you have us all staying here for long!' said Mary to her grandmother. That made them all laugh.

'Now, if you've finished, you can go,' said Granny. 'Ralph, take the twins and show them everything. They will have forgotten the way round the garden and into the farmyard.'

'Right,' said Ralph. 'Just half a minute.'

He raced upstairs, two steps at a time. He came down again in a few minutes, dressed as a Red Indian, with a magnificent tail of feathers falling from his head-dress to his feet. He really looked very grand. He had a rubber axe in his belt, and had daubed his face with coloured chalk.

'Good gracious!' said Granny. 'I shall never get used to your face looking like that!'

'You look fine,' said Bob, wishing he had a Red Indian suit like Ralph's. 'Come on – let's go out. I want to see round the garden again.'

Once out in the garden Ralph acted like a real Red Indian, startling Mary very much. He stalked beside a hedge, bent double, and then, at the end of it, leapt high into the air with a tremendous yell, flourishing his axe.

A scream came from the other side of the hedge, and then an angry voice.

'I've told you before not to jump at me like that, Ralph! Here I am, picking peas, and you've made me upset the whole basket. You come and pick the pods up for me!'

'No, thanks!' said Ralph, and stalked on, his eye on Turner, who had just appeared out of a shed.

Mary stopped by Cookie. 'I'll pick up the pods,' she said. 'Oh goodness – Ralph has pounced on Mr Turner now!'

There was a loud yell as Ralph leapt on Turner – and then another as Turner, startled, swung round and flung him off roughly. Ralph hit the ground hard, and sat up, dazed. To the twins' amazement he began to howl.

'You hurt me! You've no right to fling me about like that. I'll tell my grandmother!'

'So will I,' said Turner, grimly, and went back into the shed again. 'Cry-baby!'

Ralph got up, took a look at the twins, who stood near by feeling ashamed of him, and then ran off round a corner.

'Well, he may be big, but he's not very brave,' said Mary. 'Come on, let's go round the garden alone.'

So they went round it, peeping into corners they remembered, dabbling in the goldfish pond, looking up into a tree they used to climb, watching the ducks on the duck-pond. They

looked for eggs in the hen-house, and all the time Jiminy came round with them, his stump of a tail wagging hard.

'Everything's lovely!' said Mary. 'We'll ride Bonny tomorrow — and ask Granny if we can pick some of those ripe plums for her — and climb that tree!'

'I wish Ralph wasn't staying here too,' said Bob — and then he jumped. A voice came from behind a nearby bush.

'I heard what you said! Mean things! You're just two silly little kids!' And out leapt Ralph, flourishing his rubber axe. Oh dear — what a pity he had heard what Bob had said!

CHAPTER 5

BEFORE BREAKFAST

It was lovely to wake up the next morning and see the sun streaming in at the leaded panes of their bedroom window. The twins stared out happily. They could see a long way, over hills and fields and valleys. They could see lazy cows in the fields, and white sheep dotted about the hills.

'It's going to be a lovely day,' said Mary. 'Oh blow – there's Ralph!'

Ralph had the room next door. He was getting up and sounded as if he were pulling open all the drawers, moving half the furniture, and dropping dozens of things on the floor. He certainly was a very noisy boy!

He suddenly gave a tremendous rap on their door and yelled loudly: 'Come on, lazy-bones! Buck up! It's half-past seven.'

He then flung open the door. He was now dressed as a sailor, in long blue trousers, wide at the ankles, a blue shirt with a big sailor collar, and a sailor hat. He saluted smartly and grinned.

'However many fancy-dresses have you got?' asked Mary.

Ralph stopped smiling, and gave a scowl. 'They're not fancy-dresses. They're the real thing, only made my own size. Fancy-dresses! You don't know what you are talking about!'

He slammed the door and was gone. 'Goodness!' said Mary. 'What a boy! Come on, let's get up and go out. It's a heavenly day.'

They were soon out in the garden. They helped Cookie to feed the hens, and then took some bread to feed the ducks. A small pebble whizzed by Bob's ankles and into the pond with a splash. He turned round.

Ralph was near by, still in his sailor suit, laughing. He threw another pebble and it hit a duck on the back, making it scurry over the pond quacking.

'Don't do that,' said Mary, at once. That was a silly thing to say to Ralph, of course. He at once picked up a bigger stone and threw it into the pond, making the ducks swim away to the sides at once.

'Look here,' said Bob, stepping right up to Ralph, who was quite a head taller than he was. 'Look here, you are NOT to throw stones at the ducks. That's a mean thing to do – to hurt creatures that have never done you any harm.'

'Pooh!' said Ralph, and bent to pick up another stone. Someone leapt on him fiercely, and he fell face downwards to the ground. He felt slaps

on each side of his face and yelled loudly.

'I'll tell Granny on you, Bob! Getting me down like this! You bully! I'll tell Granny!'

He managed to get up, and glared at his attacker – and dear me, what a surprise he got! It wasn't Bob who had leapt at him and slapped him – it was Mary! A very small and angry Mary, her cheeks red, her eyes bright and hard.

'It wasn't Bob,' she said. 'It was *me*, Mary! It served you right for throwing stones at the ducks. Come along and we'll tell Granny I knocked you over and slapped you. Come on, I don't mind.'

But Ralph wasn't going to tell anyone that a small girl had attacked him and slapped him – nor was he going to tell the reason why. He went very red and looked ashamed.

'I wasn't *really* stoning the ducks,' he said. 'I only meant to startle them – they're silly creatures, anyway.'

'Well, I'll slap you again if you try any more tricks like that!' said Mary, who was never afraid to stick up for anything smaller or weaker than herself. 'Or Bob will. You're a coward! You think yourself so big and grand, dressing up and acting like a Red Indian, or a cowboy or something – and you're really just a nasty little boy and a cry-baby!'

A bell rang out. Ralph gave a feeble smile and

brushed himself down. 'All right, all right, Miss Sharp-Claws. There's the breakfast bell. We'll have to go in.'

Granny didn't know that anything had happened before breakfast, and nobody told her. They all ate their cornflakes and boiled eggs and bread and butter, and chattered away to Granny.

'I thought we would take Bonny and the pony-cart and go down to the river this morning,' said Granny. 'We could take a picnic lunch with us – and you can paddle, if you like.'

'Ooooh – let's!' said Mary, delighted. Ralph took up a spoon and banged it on the table, making Granny jump.

'Fine! GRAND!' he shouted. 'I'm a sailor to-day, and I want to get near water. Hurrah!'

'That's enough, Ralph,' said Granny. 'Put that spoon down. You're not a baby now!'

'We could have a swim!' said Bob. 'Oh Granny, it's a lovely idea of yours!'

The twins ran off in excitement after breakfast. Where were their swim-suits? Granny had unpacked for them and put them into one of the drawers. They found them and were just going downstairs when they ran into Ralph. He looked gloomy.

'What's up?' said Bob. 'Hurry, because the pony-cart is at the door already.'

'I don't want to go,' said Ralph. 'It's a silly

idea of Granny's. Let's not go.'

'But you *wanted* to!' said Bob, in surprise. 'Don't you remember how you banged the spoon on the table? Why have you changed your mind?'

Granny's voice came up the stairs. 'Come along, all of you. We're just starting. Hurry up now!'

CHAPTER 6

RALPH GETS
INTO TROUBLE

Bonny the pony was ready with the little pony-cart. They all got in, and Granny put the picnic-basket down at their feet.

'I'll drive,' said Ralph, who still looked rather gloomy. He picked up the whip, jerked the reins and they set off down the drive.

'Don't jerk Bonny's head like that,' said Granny. 'There's no need to.'

Bonny trotted merrily out of the gate and into the lane. He slowed down when he came to the hill, and Ralph cracked the whip. Bonny didn't hurry, and he flicked the little pony, making him jump.

'Give me the reins,' said Granny, at once. 'You pretend you've ridden so many horses, Ralph, but you don't even know how to treat a willing little pony pulling four people up a hill. Here, Mary – you drive him.'

Mary took the reins, and Bonny felt the difference in handling at once. He went well up the hill, and then Bob had a turn. Ralph sat looking gloomy again, kicking his foot against the side of the cart.

'Cheer up, Ralph,' said Granny. 'You look like one of my hens left out in the rain.'

That made them all laugh. Ralph cheered up and began to boast. 'I've been up in an aeroplane,' he said to the twins. 'I bet *you* haven't! And I've been on the biggest liner in the world! And I've seen the Niagara Falls crashing down like thunder. One of these days I'm going to go over those falls in a boat. I've seen real Red Indians – and chased them too. And I've . . .'

'Keep to the truth, Ralph,' said Granny. 'We all know you've travelled a great deal – but we none of us believe that you ever chased Red Indians.'

'Look – there's the river away across those fields!' said Mary, in delight. 'Isn't it blue? How long will it take us to get to it, Granny?'

'About twenty minutes,' said Granny. 'Dear me, where is my sunshade? I didn't think the sun would be so hot. You *will* enjoy a paddle, my dears!'

'We've brought our swim-suits,' said Bob. 'Daddy taught us to swim last year. I can do breast-stroke, side-stroke and backstroke, Granny.'

'Well done!' said Granny. 'What can *you* do, Ralph?'

'Oh, I can do all those, and the crawl too. Easy!' said Ralph. 'I can swim under water as well. I swam under longer than anyone else last year. I can life-save too.'

'Well, you are big and strong,' said Granny. 'You should be able to life-save splendidly.'

'Let's paddle first,' said Mary. 'Then swim. Then have our picnic. And then could we have a boat, Granny? Rowing is easy, isn't it, Ralph?'

'Oh yes!' said Ralph. 'So is sailing. I sailed a fine big boat all by myself last year.'

'Did you really?' said Bob, impressed. 'My daddy hasn't taught us sailing yet. Only rowing.'

They came to the river and settled Granny in a nice shady spot under a tree. Then they all took off their shoes and socks and paddled in the cool water. It was lovely!

'Paddling's better than swimming any day!' said Ralph suddenly. 'Let's not bother to swim.'

'Oh, but we must!' said Mary. 'I love swimming – and perhaps you could teach us the crawl, Ralph. We don't know it.'

Ralph looked gloomy again, and gloomier still when Bob went to put on his swim-suit. Then he suddenly called out: 'Goodness me – I've forgotten my swim-suit! I can't go in to swim after all – what a pity!'

'Well, look – I've brought *two* suits!' said Bob, generously. 'I thought I'd wear one this morning and another dry one this afternoon – but you can have it. It will be a bit small, that's all.'

'Oh no – I don't want to wear your suit,' said Ralph – and then he heard Granny's voice.

'For goodness' sake put on Bob's second suit!' she called. 'A swim will do you good!' So Ralph put it on, looking very cross.

They all went into the water. Ralph went in up to his waist, and stood there, shivering. Bob and Mary dived under and came up, swimming strongly and well. Granny clapped them, delighted.

'Go in, Ralph, go in!' she cried. Bob swam up behind him, dived down and caught his legs. Into the water went Ralph, right over his head. He came up spluttering and screaming:

'You'll drown me, you'll drown me!'

Bob stared at him in surprise. 'Well, swim then, silly – go on! Show us how to do the crawl.'

But Ralph merely stood there, shivering and looking miserable. Mary swam up to him and stood up. '*I* know what's the matter with you!' she said. 'You *can't* swim, Ralph! *That's* why you left your swim-suit behind. That's why you didn't want to come. Baby!'

'You horrid girl!' cried Ralph, and tried to

slap Mary. He stumbled forward, stepped into a suddenly deep place, and went under the water.

'Save him!' yelled Mary. 'It's deep here, Bob. Save him!'

So Bob had to life-save poor Ralph, and drag him to shore, kicking and howling with fright. Dear, dear, what a to-do!

'For goodness' sake, let's have lunch!' said Granny. 'And if Ralph doesn't stop howling I'll try slapping — I believe that is quite good for people who think they have been half-drowned!'

And, as you can guess, the great sailor-man was quiet at once. How the others laughed!

CHAPTER 7

THE END OF THE DAY

The picnic went off very well, once Ralph became sensible again. He certainly ate a great deal. Granny said she didn't know where he put it all!

'Now what about a boat?' said Granny, after the picnic. 'Do you want to go rowing?'

'Oh *yes*,' said Bob and Mary. Granny turned to Ralph.

'You said you knew all about rowing and sailing. *Do* you? Because I am not going to let anyone go out in a boat unless they really know about boats – especially someone who can't swim.'

'Well – I don't know *very* much,' said Ralph, going rather red.

'That's just what I thought,' said Granny. 'You stay here with me, then – and you, Bob, go to the boatman's cottage down there, and get his little boat for yourself and Mary.'

Soon the twins were rowing back to Granny.
Ralph, looking fine in his sailor-boy suit, sat and
watched them sulkily. *He* ought to be rowing –
he was dressed as a sailor, wasn't he? And yet he
couldn't swim or manage even a small boat. He
felt very small.

They went back home to tea, tired out, sun-
burnt, and the twins very happy, though Ralph
was still sulky.

'Oh, I'm quite tired with all my rowing and
swimming,' said Mary, flinging herself down on
the lawn after tea.

'Have a book, and read it quietly,' said
Granny.

'Oooh yes – we've brought some exciting ones
away with us,' said Bob, remembering. 'I'll get
them. They are all about seven children who
make a Secret Society and have adventures.'

He brought out three books and gave one to
Ralph. 'Here you are – *Secret Seven Adventure*, he
said. 'I'll lend it to you.'

'I'd rather go and climb trees,' said Ralph. But
Granny wouldn't let him, so he opened the book
sulkily. The other two settled into theirs, and
there was a silence that Granny quite enjoyed.
Then suddenly Ralph shut his book.

'I've finished it,' he said. 'Now can I go and
climb trees, Granny?'

'You can't *possibly* have finished it,' said Granny. 'You know you haven't! You can't climb trees. Sit and do nothing – or read your book properly.'

'I tell you I've read it all,' said Ralph. 'I read quickly – not slowly like Mary there – she takes ages to turn a page!'

'Be quiet. I want to read,' said Bob, and Ralph said no more. Soon Granny fell asleep, and Ralph nudged Bob.

'I'm going to climb trees,' he whispered. 'I can't sit here and read any more.'

'You haven't read a word. I don't believe you *can* read!' said Bob.

'I can! I can read very difficult words – and very fast too!' said Ralph. 'Don't wake Granny. I'm off!'

And he crept away to where the trees grew in a little thicket at the bottom of the garden. Bob and Mary let him go. They were tired of him!

Granny woke up and looked at her watch. 'Good gracious! It's time for bed. Where's that boy Ralph? If he has gone to climb trees I shall be very cross.'

They all three went indoors. Ralph was not to be seen. And then, just as Bob and Mary were getting undressed, yells came from down the garden.

'Help! Help! Come and help me!'

Bob pulled on his shirt again and tore down the stairs, with Mary following him. They went to the bottom of the garden, where the yells came from. Turner was there as well, grinning all over his face.

'*Here's* a clever boy!' he said. 'Climbs trees like a monkey – and then is afraid to get down! No one is going to climb up to you – so come on down!'

'Fetch a ladder!' called Ralph. 'I've torn my sailor shirt already. Get me a ladder.'

But Turner wouldn't – and in the end Ralph had to slither down by himself, scratching his hands, and tearing his trousers as well as his shirt. Granny was very cross with him when at last he came in.

'Go and have a bath – and tomorrow please put on an ordinary pair of shorts and a shirt,' she said. 'Wait till you are braver and more sensible, before you parade about as a Red Indian, or cowboy or sailor!'

Poor Ralph went to bed without any supper. He said he couldn't eat any because he felt sick, but Bob was sure it was because he couldn't bear to be scolded in front of the twins.

It was a nice supper too – stuffed eggs and jam tarts to follow. Mary was most surprised to see that Bob had taken two stuffed eggs and four jam tarts. How greedy!

But he had one of the eggs and two of the tarts for Ralph! Ralph was silly and he didn't like him, but Bob knew how horrid it is to go without supper. It is such a very long time till breakfast if you don't have supper.

Ralph was surprised and very grateful. 'Oh *thanks*!' he said. 'You *are* a friend. I say – it looks as if it's going to rain tonight, doesn't it? What a shame! I don't want to stay indoors all day.'

'Oh, it may be fine again tomorrow,' said Bob. 'Goodnight – and don't dream about swimming, or you'll wake up drowning!'

He went off to his room and looked out of the window. It was pouring with rain. Bother. It would be so dull staying indoors all day. But it wasn't dull. It turned out to be really very exciting!

CHAPTER 8

Granny Sets a
Few Puzzles

The next day was dark and rainy. The sun was hidden behind thick clouds, and Granny wondered what to do with the children.

'I'll set you a few puzzles,' she said. 'And the prize shall be a box of chocolates. Here's the first puzzle. Go into the dining-room, and have a good look round. Count all the clawed feet you can see there, and come back and tell me the number. Then I'll set you a few more puzzles.'

'Oh, I know *four* clawed feet there!' said Ralph. 'The stuffed fox!'

'Don't give things away!' said Mary. They went into the dining-room and looked around. Yes – stuffed fox – and a stuffed hawk with clawed feet. And a picture of an owl, he had clawed feet too.

Bob noticed a little statue of a lion on the

mantelpiece – four more clawed feet. He wondered if the others would notice it.

A bell rang after a time. That was to say they were to come back and report to Granny. 'Well,' she said, when they arrived. 'How many clawed feet did *you* see, Ralph?'

'I bet I got the most!' said Ralph. 'I counted twelve – fox, owl, hawk and lion!'

'I got those twelve too,' said Bob.

'I got *forty-four* clawed feet!' said Mary, almost crowing in delight.

'You didn't!' said Ralph. 'What are they?'

'Lion, fox, owl, hawk – and the table has four clawed feet, and so have each of the chairs, and the sideboard!' said Mary.

'Right!' said Granny. 'They are old chairs and table – the kind that have carved legs holding a ball in the claws of the foot. Well done, Mary.'

'Jolly good!' said Bob. 'What's the next puzzle, Granny?'

'Go into the drawing-room and count all the roses you can see,' said Granny. So off they ran.

'Fourteen roses in that vase – and sixteen in this one – and a rose embroidered on that cushion – and another on the fire-screen,' thought Mary. 'Any on the carpet? No. Any on the curtains? No!'

They were soon back again. 'Mary, how many?' said Granny.

'Thirty-two,' said Mary.

'Thirty-one,' said Ralph, who had counted the ones in the vases wrongly.

'*Sixty*-two!' said Bob, proudly. And he was right! 'I looked up at the ceiling, Granny, and it had roses carved on it,' he explained. Granny nodded.

'Yes – those roses were carved long ago. You were clever to notice them. Now – one last puzzle. In the gallery upstairs there are portraits of six women who lived in the olden days – great-great-great-grandmothers of yours and mine. In five of their pictures appears the same thing. I want you to tell me what it is.'

The children ran off to the gallery. It was dark up there and Bob switched on the lights. The big portraits looked down on them from the walls, most of them dark and dingy for they were very old. There were both men and women, and the children picked out the six women and looked at them carefully.

'I know, I know!' cried Mary and ran downstairs to Granny. The two boys stared and stared at the six pictures but all the women in them wore different dresses, different collars, different cuffs. Nothing in the pictures seemed the same. They gave it up.

'What's the answer, Mary?' asked Granny, when the boys joined them downstairs.

'The necklace!' said Mary. 'I could hardly see it in the first two portraits – but it was quite clear in the third one – and half-hidden under the collar of the fourth one – and shone out in the fifth one – but it wasn't in the sixth picture.'

'Yes. Quite right. You shall have the box of chocolates,' said Granny. 'Here it is.'

'Granny, have *you* got that old necklace?' asked Mary. 'Was it a kind of family necklace?'

'Yes, it was,' said Granny. 'It was a magnificent one, made of pearls, and each of the women who lived in this house wore it. But I can't wear it, because it disappeared about a hundred years ago.'

'How?' asked Mary, handing round the chocolates.

'Well, it's supposed to be hidden somewhere in this house,' said Granny. 'But people have looked everywhere, as you can guess – so I fear it must have been stolen. How I should have loved to wear it! It ought to go to your own mother, after me, Mary – but it will never be found now.'

'We'll look for it!' cried Bob. 'A treasure-hunt! Who's for a treasure-hunt! This very afternoon!'

'We are, we are!' shouted Mary and Ralph. Mary turned to Granny. 'Granny, is there a plan of the house anywhere?'

'There may be, in one of the old books in the

study,' said Granny. 'They haven't been opened for years, and are as dull as can be. But you *might* find a plan of the house if you can find a history of it — there should be one or two books about it.'

So, that afternoon, three excited children went to the study and began taking down the old books there. How dusty and dull they were — and what strange printing they had!

'Here's one about Granny's house, Tall Chimneys, look!' said Bob, at last. 'Now — let's see if there's a plan of the house — it might show secret passages or something. Ooooh look — there *is* a plan!'

CHAPTER 9

THE OLD, OLD BOOK

The three children bent over the old book. It was a history of Tall Chimneys, Granny's house. At the beginning of it were some strange old maps.

'This one shows the grounds,' said Bob. 'And this one shows the two farms. And this one – what's this one?'

They pored over the yellowed map. 'It's the cellars of the house!' said Mary, pointing to an oddly printed word. 'What's the next map?'

Bob turned over the page. 'This plan seems to be of the ground floor,' he said. 'Yes, look – this very room we are sitting in is marked – it says "Library". Isn't it peculiar to think that people sat in this very place, hundreds of years ago, perhaps looking at this same book!'

Mary was peering closely at the map. She had seen something strange – at least, it seemed strange to her. 'Look!' she said. 'There's a little door marked in the wall here – in the plan, see – but *I* can't see one in the real room we're in, can you?'

'Only the door we came in by – and that is marked on the plan too, in its right place,' said Bob, excited. 'Quick! Let's see if there is a secret door we haven't noticed in the wall over there!'

The walls had bookcases all round them. The children tried to move out the great shelves that hid the wall where a door was shown in the plan. But they couldn't. It really was terribly disappointing.

'Let's go and tell Granny,' said Mary.

'No. We just *might* find the door somehow and, who knows, we might find a hiding-place behind it where the necklace was put for safety – perhaps during a war or something,' said Bob, his face red with excitement.

Mary ran through the pages of the old book, hoping to find other maps. Two words suddenly caught her eye. 'Secret Passage'! It was a wonder she saw them, because they were printed in old-fashioned letters, and the letter *S* was just like *f*! She put her finger on the words at once, afraid she would lose them.

'Look – there must be something about the secret door on this page!' she said. 'I just noticed "Secret Passage"! I expect the door leads into it.

Oh dear – can we possibly read this funny old printing?'

Bob read the words out slowly. 'The – Secret – Passage was – made, er – er . . .'

Mary went on. 'Was made – when – the house – was – er, was built. The door – to it – leads – er – leads from the – library. It . . .'

'Isn't this *thrilling*!' said Bob. They read the whole page slowly – and on it were the directions for moving the big bookcase and getting at the door!

'I *say* – if we follow these directions, we can get through that door and see where the secret passage goes to!' said Bob, his eyes shining. 'What an adventure!'

They took the old book to the big bookcase. Mary tried to read the first direction, but it was so very dark in that corner that she couldn't. She gave the book to Ralph.

'Now you take the page over to the window and read out the directions to us one by one,' she said. 'That will be a help. Bob and I will do what the directions say. I remember the first one – take out the fifth book.'

'Yes – but from what shelf?' said Bob. 'Hey, Ralph! What shelf do we have to take the fifth book from? Buck up, silly! Can't you read what's printed there? We've read it out loud once already!'

'Er – the fifth book,' repeated Ralph, his eyes on the book. 'From the – er – the ninth shelf.'

'Ninth shelf. Let's count,' said Mary, and they counted. 'It's pretty high up,' she said. 'We'd better get the ladder.'

So they went to the kitchen and got the little ladder. They wouldn't tell Cookie what they wanted it for, and were really very mysterious about it!

They took it to the study – and just then the tea-bell rang. How very annoying!

'Well – we'll come back at once, after tea,' said Bob. 'Now – not a word to Granny. We'll find out simply everything and then give her a grand surprise.'

So they didn't tell Granny and talked about all sorts of other things. But just now and then Bob nudged Mary and smiled at her, and she knew what he meant. 'What fun we're going to have after tea!'

They went back to the study afterwards, and put the ladder against the ninth shelf. Bob climbed up while Mary held the ladder. Ralph watched.

'Ninth shelf,' said Bob. 'Wait a minute – I must know if the fifth book has to be taken from the right of the shelf or the left. Ralph, look up the directions and see. Take the book to the window again.'

Ralph pored over the page. Bob grew impatient. 'Oh for goodness' sake, buck up, Ralph. What does it say? Right or left?'

'Er – right,' said Ralph. 'Sorry. I lost the place.'

In excitement Bob took the fifth book from the right of the ninth shelf. He gave it to Mary. Then he put his hand into the gap left by the book, and felt about there. What would he find? A handle? A knob to turn? A lever to pull? It was too exciting for words!

CHAPTER 10

A QUARREL

'Can you feel anything there?' asked Mary. 'Quick, tell us!'

'I can't feel a thing!' said Bob, disappointed. 'Not a thing! Wait, I'll take a few more books out and see.'

He handed down a few books to Mary and then felt around at the back of the shelf again. No – there was nothing there – no knob, no handle, nothing!

'You come up and try, Mary,' said Bob, at last. He climbed down, his hands black with dust.

'Let's just count the shelves again to make sure we've got the ninth,' said Mary. They counted – and found that they had been right before. The shelf that Bob had been looking along was certainly the ninth.

Then Mary went up the ladder and felt all along the shelf, sliding the books to and fro so that she could reach. Bob moved the ladder when she could reach no further.

'Nothing!' said Mary. 'It's too disappointing for words. Ralph, have a turn.'

Ralph went up, but, of course, he couldn't find anything either! The three children looked at one another, frowning. Now what could be done?

Mary went to the window and picked up the old book, which Ralph had put down on the broad wooden sill. She read down the page – and then she gave a sudden squeal.

'It *isn't* the ninth shelf – it's the *fifth*! It says so quite clearly. And it's the fifth book we're to move, as we thought – but it's the fifth on the *left*, not the right, as you said, Ralph. Why did you tell us wrong?'

Ralph said nothing. He just scowled. Bob lost his temper and stamped his foot.

'You're mean! Yes, mean, mean, MEAN! You told us wrong so that we wouldn't find the secret door – and you meant to find it yourself when we weren't here.'

'I didn't,' said Ralph.

'You did, you did! It's just like you. You gave us wrong directions – and knew we wouldn't find the door. But we shall, see. And we'll turn you out of this study and lock the door so that you won't be here to see!'

Bob gave Ralph a rough push, but he stood his ground. 'No, don't! I want to see the secret door. I tell you I didn't mean to find it by myself without you. I tell you I . . .'

'We don't believe a word!' said Mary. 'Not a single word. You boast and you tell stories and you pretend to be so big and bold – but all the time you're mean – and a cry-baby too. We won't *let* you find the secret door with us! Go out of the room!'

'I shan't,' said Ralph. 'I'm bigger than either of you, and I won't go out. So there!'

Bob and Mary began to push and shove him and Ralph shoved back. They all fell over in a heap – and at that very moment Granny put her head in at the study door.

'What *are* you doing? Haven't you heard the bell to tell you it's bedtime? At least, it's *almost* bedtime, but I thought you'd like me to tell you a story first.'

'You tell it to Bob and Mary, Granny,' said Ralph, quickly. 'I don't want to hear one tonight.'

Bob glared at him. He knew quite well what was in Ralph's mind. He was going to find that secret door while he and Mary were listening to Granny! Just like him! But how could Bob stop him, unless he told Granny everything? And he did so want to keep it all a secret!

'Well, if you don't want to hear the story, Ralph, you can go up and run the bath-water,' said Granny, much to the twins' relief. 'I know you like doing that. But if you let it go above half-way I shall be very cross with you. I'm not going to have the bathroom swimming in water, like last week!'

Ralph went off, frowning. Now he wouldn't be able to stay in the study on his own. Still, the others would be hearing a story, and *they* wouldn't be able to do any exploring either! He cheered up a little and went to turn on the taps.

He wondered if he would have time to slip down to the study while the bath was filling.

'No, I'd better not,' he thought. 'I might get excited and forget the bath-water – and Granny might quite well tell me off if the floor gets flooded again. But I'll be sure to keep close to the others all day tomorrow, so that they can't find that secret door without me!'

Granny told the twins a story, then kissed them and sent them up to bed. 'I'll be up in a minute,' she said, 'and I'll bring your supper – bananas and cream. Begin to get undressed, and tell Ralph I'm just coming. He's probably sailing his boat in the bath.'

He was. He wouldn't speak to the twins when they came up, and they didn't speak to him either, except to say that Granny was soon coming. They were soon all in bed, eating sliced bananas and cream, with sugar all over the plate – lovely!

Granny tucked them in, said goodnight and left the twins in their room. Then she went to tuck Ralph in too.

Bob began to whisper to Mary. 'Mary, listen! If we leave everything till tomorrow it will be very difficult to find the door without Ralph being there – and I *won't* let him share in this now – so what about trying to find it tonight, when Granny is in bed?'

'Oh *yes*!' said Mary, thrilled. 'Yes, Bob! We'll keep awake till we hear Granny going to bed – and then we'll creep down to the study. Oh! *What* an adventure!'

CHAPTER 11

IN THE MIDDLE
OF THE NIGHT

Granny had some friends to see her that night. They stayed late, and it was difficult for the children to keep awake. In the end they took it in turns to keep awake for half-an-hour, sleeping soundly in between.

At last Bob, who was the one awake, heard the cars leaving the front door, and heard Granny coming upstairs. Click – click – click! That was the electric lights being turned off. Now, except for a light on the landing outside, and in Granny's room, the house was in darkness.

Bob woke up Mary. 'The visitors have gone,' he whispered. 'And Granny has come up to bed. Let's put on our slippers and dressing-gowns and go down. Granny won't hear us or see us now she's in her bedroom.'

Mary leapt out of her bed, wide awake with excitement. She switched on her torch, and put on her slippers and dressing-gown. 'My fingers are shaking!' she whispered to Bob. 'Oh Bob – isn't this thrilling?'

They went down the stairs very cautiously, and came into the big hall. The moon shone in through the window there, and lit up every corner. Mary was glad. She didn't like pitch-black shadows!

They went into the study. The moon shone through the windows there too, and showed them the ladder still up by the big bookcase. They went to it.

'Now – the fifth book on the fifth shelf, counting from the left,' said Bob. He went up the ladder, and then came down again. 'I can reach the fifth shelf easily, without using the ladder!' he said, and pushed it aside.

He took out the fifth book from the left of the fifth shelf and gave it to Mary. Then he began to feel about at the back of the gap where the book had stood. Mary stood watching him, trembling in excitement, trying to shine her torch where it would best help Bob.

He gave a little cry. 'Mary! There's something here – a sort of knob. I'm twisting it – no, it won't twist. I'll pull it – oh it's moved!'

There was a noise as he pulled the knob, and then another noise – a creaking, groaning noise. The bookcase suddenly seemed to push against

Bob, and he stepped back surprised.

The whole case was moving slowly out from the wall, leaving a small space behind it of about a foot. The knob worked some lever that pushed the bookcase forward in a most ingenious way! Mary stared, holding her breath. How strange!

'The secret door will be behind the bookcase!' said Bob, forgetting to whisper in his excitement. 'I'll squeeze behind and see if I can find it.'

He squeezed himself behind, shining his torch on the wooden panelling. Mary heard him take a sudden breath. 'Yes! it *is* here, Mary! The old, old secret door! It must be years and years since anyone went through it.'

'Can you open it?' asked Mary, her voice trembling. 'Oh Bob!'

Bob was feeling all over the small door, which appeared to be cut out of the panelling. His fingers came to a little hole and he poked his first finger through it. It touched something, and there was a click as if a latch had fallen.

The door swung open suddenly and silently in front of Bob. A little dark passage was behind, and Bob shone his torch into it. 'Mary! Come on! I've got the door open and it leads into the Secret Passage. Let's see where it goes. Come on!'

Mary squeezed herself behind the bookcase to the open door. It was no higher than her head.

Bob was already in the passage, and he held out his hand to her.

'Come on. It goes upwards here, in steep steps, behind the panelling. Hold my hand.'

It was dark and musty in the passage, and in one or two places they had to bend their heads because the roof was so low. It seemed to be a secret way behind the panelled walls of the study – but as the steps went on and on upwards Bob guessed they must now be behind the walls of some room upstairs.

The passage suddenly turned to the left, and then instead of going upwards ran level. It came to a sudden end at another door – a sturdy one this time, studded with big nails. It had a handle on the outside in the shape of a big iron ring, and Bob turned it.

The door opened into a tiny room, so tiny that it could only hold a wooden stool, a little wooden table, and a narrow bench on which there was an old, rotten blanket.

A wooden bowl stood on the table, and a tumbler made of thick glass. They could see nothing else inside the room at all.

'This is an old hidey-hole,' said Bob, almost too thrilled to speak. 'I wonder how many people have hidden here from their enemies, at one time or another? Look, there's even an old blanket left here by the last person.'

'There's no sign of the necklace,' said Mary, shining her torch round the tiny room. 'But look, Bob – what's that – in the wall there?'

'A cupboard – a very rough one,' said Bob. 'Not much more than a hole in the wall. Give me the stool, Mary. I'll stand on it and shine my torch inside!'

He stood on the stool, and peered into the hole, holding his torch to light him. He gave a cry and almost fell off the stool.

'Quick! Get up and look, Mary! Oh *quick*!'

CHAPTER 12

THE HIDEY-HOLE

Mary pushed Bob off the stool and stood on it herself, her heart beating fast in excitement. She shone her torch into the hole. At once something sparkled brilliantly, and flashed in the torchlight!

'Bob! Is it the necklace?' she cried. 'Oh *Bob*!'

'You can be the one to take it out,' said Bob. 'Be careful of it now – remember it may be worth thousands of pounds!'

Half-fearfully Mary put in her hand. She took hold of the sparkling mass, and gave a squeal.

'There are *lots* of things – not only a necklace. A bracelet – and rings – and brooches – oh, they're *beautiful*, Bob!'

'Hand them out to me one by one,' said Bob. 'Carefully now. Oh Mary – what*ever* will Granny say?'

Mary handed Bob the things – a bracelet that

shone like fire with red rubies — another one that glittered with diamonds — rings with stones of all sizes and shapes — brooches — and last of all the magnificent pearlj78

necklace that the twins had seen round the necks of the five women in the portraits! Yes — there was no doubt of it — this was the long-lost necklace!

Bob put everything in his dressing-gown pocket. It was the only place he could put them in. They felt quite heavy there!

'Now let's go and wake Granny!' he said, as Mary got off the stool. He shone his torch on the door, which had closed behind them. 'Come on, Mary. I wonder what Ralph will say when he knows we've got the jewellery!'

'I don't care *what* he says!' said Mary. 'He didn't deserve to share in our adventure because of his meanness in reading us out the wrong directions!'

Bob was trying to open the door. 'It's funny — there's no handle this side,' he said. 'I wonder how it opens?'

He pushed it, but it wouldn't move. He pulled it and shook it, but it didn't open. He kicked it, but it stayed firmly shut.

Mary suddenly felt frightened. 'I say, Bob — wouldn't it be dreadful if we couldn't get it open? Would we have to stay here for ever?'

'Don't be so silly! Somebody would find the bookcase was moved, and would explore and discover the secret door, and come up the passage and find us,' said Bob.

'But I don't want to be here all night!' wailed Mary. 'I don't like it – and my torch is getting very weak. I hope yours is all right. I don't want to be here all in the dark.'

'I shall look after you,' said Bob, firmly. 'You know that brothers always look after their sisters. Just think of all the lovely treasures we've got tonight, Mary. What about putting everything on? That will help you to pass the time.'

Mary thought that was a very good idea, and soon she was gleaming brightly as she put on brooches, bracelets, rings and necklace! The rings were too large so she had to close her hands to keep them from falling off.

'You look wonderful!' said Bob, shining his torch on Mary. 'Like a princess!'

Suddenly they heard a noise, and Mary clutched at Bob. 'What was that?' she whispered. 'Did you hear it?'

The noise came again. A kind of shuffling noise – was it somebody coming up the passage? Who could it be? Surely nobody lived in this little secret room?

The twins stood absolutely still, hardly daring to breathe – and then they heard a familiar voice.

'Hey! Bob! Mary! Are you here?'

'Ralph!' yelled the twins, feeling extremely glad to hear his voice. 'Yes, we're here – but we can't open the door from this side. Open it from your side, will you?'

Ralph turned the handle outside and the door opened! He looked in, shining his torch. When he saw Mary, sparkling and glittering in the beam of his torch, his mouth fell open in surprise. He could hardly say a word.

'Oh!' he said at last. 'So you found the necklace then! You *might* have waited for me, Bob.'

'I like *that*!' said Bob. 'You weren't going to wait for *us*, were you? You've got up in the middle of the night to come and explore all by yourself, haven't you? And you found that we were before you!'

'No. No, Bob, you're wrong,' said Ralph earnestly. 'I couldn't go to sleep tonight, because I was worried that you thought I was so mean – you thought I'd given you wrong directions on purpose –'

'Well, didn't you?' demanded Bob.

'No,' said Ralph. 'No, I didn't. You see – I'm not good at reading. I can't read at all to myself, really, unless it's very very easy – but I was ashamed to tell you I couldn't read those words in the old book – and I just said what I thought, and it was wrong, of course.'

There was silence for a minute. 'I see,' said Bob at last. 'So you didn't even read that book after tea yesterday – the one you seemed to finish so quickly. You do tell dreadful stories, Ralph.'

'I know. The thing is – I'm so big that people expect me to know a lot and I don't,' said Ralph. 'So I pretend, you see. And I was sorry tonight and I came to your room to tell you – but you were gone!'

'So you followed us,' said Mary. 'Well, I'm very glad you did, Ralph, or we'd have been here all night. I'm sorry we called you mean. We really and truly thought you read out wrong directions on purpose to stop us finding the door.'

'I'm sorry too,' said Bob, and solemnly held out his hand. The boys shook hands.

'I missed the adventure,' said Ralph, sorrowfully.

'Never mind – you came in at the end of it,' said Mary. 'Now – let's go and wake Granny!'

CHAPTER 25

The End of the Adventure

The three children left the tiny hidey-hole behind them, and went in single file down the secret passage. They came at last to the little secret door that led into the study, behind the bookcase.

The moon still shone through the windows and Mary's jewellery sparkled even more brilliantly. The boys thought she looked lovely!

They went quietly up the stairs to Granny's bedroom, and knocked on the door.

'Who's there?' said Granny's voice, sleepily.

'It's us – the twins and Ralph,' said Bob.

'What's the matter? Is one of you ill?' called Granny. 'Come in – the door isn't locked.'

They heard a click as Granny put on her light. They opened the door and went in, still in their slippers and dressing-gowns.

Granny looked at them anxiously, thinking

that one of them at least must be ill. She suddenly saw all the glittering jewellery that Mary had on.

'Mary! What have you got on? Where did you get all that?' she began. Then she saw the necklace. 'Mary – that necklace! Good gracious, am I dreaming, or is that the lost necklace? I *must* be dreaming!'

'You're not, Granny,' said Mary, coming close to the bed. 'It *is* the lost necklace – look, it's the same one that is painted in all those portraits – with the big shiny pearls and everything!'

'My dear child!' said Granny, in wonder, and put out her hand to touch the sparkling pearls. 'But these rings – and brooches – where *did* you find them? Sit on my bed and tell me. I can't wait to hear!'

So the three of them cuddled into Granny's soft eiderdown, and told their strange story – all about the plans in the old book – the mention of the passage and the directions for finding the secret door – and the hidey-hole where, most unexpectedly, they had found the jewellery in the little cubby-hole in the wall.

'I just can't believe it!' Granny kept saying. 'I just can't. To think it was there, in a place that every single person had forgotten through all these years! And all these other treasures too. How I wish I knew the story of why they were

hidden there – some thief, I suppose, stole them and put them in the safest place he knew – and then couldn't get to them again!'

'Will they be yours, all these things, Granny?' asked Mary.

'The necklace certainly will, because it belongs to the family,' said Granny, 'and I expect the other things will too. Look, this ruby ring is the one painted on the finger of the third woman in the gallery of pictures!'

So it was. Mary remembered it quite well. She took off all the sparkling jewellery carefully and handed it to Granny.

'That was a real adventure, wasn't it, Granny?' she said.

'It certainly was. Did you enjoy it too, Ralph?' asked Granny.

'Yes,' said Ralph, hoping that the twins wouldn't tell that he had only come in at the last. They didn't say a word. They were very sorry that Ralph *hadn't* shared all the adventure now. They felt much more kindly towards him, now they knew why he boasted and told such silly stories.

'You must go back to bed,' said Granny, at last. 'We'll talk about it all again tomorrow. It's too exciting for words!'

Everyone in the house was thrilled to hear about the midnight adventure. Cookie, who had been called by Mrs Hughes, the housekeeper, early next morning to see the bookcase out of its place, just couldn't believe it all.

'Well, well – it isn't often we have an adventure like this happening in Tall Chimneys!' she said. 'I'll have to make a special cake to celebrate it!'

So she did – and she actually made a beautiful necklace all round the cake, in white icing. It really was clever of her.

'Well, you will find the rest of your stay here rather dull, I'm afraid, after all this excitement,' said Granny, when they sat down to their lunch in the middle of the day.

'No, we shan't,' said Mary. 'We're going to have a jolly good time with Ralph – aren't we, Bob? We're going to teach him to swim, and to row – and lots of other things!'

Ralph beamed. 'Yes. I shan't need to show off and pretend then. Don't you worry, Granny – we're going to have a *grand* time here – and I expect I'll be a lot nicer than I've been before.'

'That's good news,' said Granny. 'You haven't always been nice, but I shall expect great things of you now.'

They did have a grand time together, and Ralph learnt a whole lot of things he didn't know before. The twins began to like him very much indeed.

Before they left Tall Chimneys, they all had a surprise. Granny said she wanted to give them goodbye presents.

'This is for you, Mary,' she said, and gave the little girl a small sparkling brooch that had been in the lost jewellery. 'I've had it cleaned and altered – and now it is just right for a little girl like you to wear at a party.'

She turned to the boys. 'And I've sold a little of the jewellery I didn't want to keep,' she said, 'and I have bought these watches, one for each of you – just to remind you of the adventure you had at Granny's!'

She gave them two splendid watches, and they put them on proudly. What would the boys at school say when they saw *those*?

'Thank you, Granny!' said the children, and hugged her. 'We've had a simply lovely time – and we never never *will* forget our Adventure of the Secret Necklace.'

Enid Blyton titles available at Bloomsbury Children's Books

Adventure!
Mischief at St Rollo's
The Children of Kidillin
The Secret of Cliff Castle
Smuggler Ben
The Boy Who Wanted a Dog

Happy Days!
The Adventures of Mr Pink-Whistle
Run-About's Holiday
Bimbo and Topsy
Hello Mr Twiddle
Shuffle the Shoemaker
Mr Meddle's Mischief
Snowball the Pony
The Adventures of Binkle and Flip

Enid Blyton Age-Ranged Story Collections
Best Stories for Five-Year-Olds
Best Stories for Six-Year-Olds
Best Stories for Seven-Year-Olds
Best Stories for Eight-Year-Olds

WIN A WEEKEND BREAK
FOR YOUR FAMILY AT CENTER PARCS

THE COMPETITION WILL BE JUDGED BY ENID BLYTON'S DAUGHTER,
GILLIAN BAVERSTOCK, AND THE FIVE LUCKY WINNERS WILL BE
ANNOUNCED ON THE 19TH AUGUST 1997.

HOW TO ENTER

1. Solve the riddle:

   My first is in apple and also in pear
   My second's in rabbit but never in hare
   My third is in lucky but not in thirteen
   My fourth is in runner and also in bean   _____
   My fifth is in tortoise and also in snail
   My last is in bucket but never in pail
   My whole is a pleasure to go on together
   But better watch out for the wasps and the weather!

2. Now describe the most amazing adventure you've ever had
   (using no more than 30 words):

   _____

   _____

   _____

   _____

   _____

   _____

Please send your entries on this form to the following address:
Blyton/Center Parcs Competition
Bloomsbury Publishing Plc, 38 Soho Square, London W1V 5DF.

Name: _____ Age: _____

Address: _____

_____

Telephone Number: _____

Signature of a parent/responsible adult: _____

The competition is open to any child of twelve years and under and resident in the U.K.
All entries must be signed by a parent or guardian.
See overleaf for Terms and Conditions.

CLOSING DATE FOR ENTRIES: 31ST JULY 1997.

Terms and Conditions

1. Bloomsbury Publishing Plc cannot take any responsibility for the return of any entries to the competition.

2. The competition is open to any child of twelve years and under and resident in the U.K, subject to signature of parent or guardian. No employees of Bloomsbury Publishing Plc, Center Parcs or their agents are eligible to enter the competition.

3. The prizes for winning entries will be the ones specified only. They may not be changed and are non-transferable. No substitute prizes or cash alternatives are available. The prizes consist of the use of a 3-bedroom villa for a family of up to 6 at a UK Center Parcs Village, plus £150 worth of Center Parcs' vouchers which can be spent in the Village. It does not include any additional charges such as meals, insurance, sports & leisure activities or other personal expenses. Travel expenses are covered up to the value of £50 per prize. Bookings are subject to availability and to the terms and conditions published in Center Parcs' brochure.
   The prizes should be taken by Spring 1998.

4. All entries must be received by 31st July1997. All entries must be submitted using this competition page, photocopies will not be accepted. Incomplete, illegible, spoilt or late entries will not be considered.

5. The prizes will be awarded to the entrants who have correctly solved the riddle and, in the judge's opinion, have submitted the most apt, original and amazing adventure. All entries will be judged by Gillian Baverstock. Her decision is final and no correspondence will be entered into.

6. Winners will be notified by post or telephone, no later than Monday 11th August. The winners will be required to attend a party on 19th August 1997 to announce the prizes to the press, they may also be required to attend picture-taking for publicity purposes without compensation, other than reasonable out of pocket expenses.

7. Details of winners and results will be available by post after 11th August. If required please send a stamped, self-addressed envelope to Blyton/Center Parcs Competition, Bloomsbury Publishing Plc, 38 Soho Square, London, W1V 5DF.

8. All entry instructions form part of the rules and the submission of an entry will be deemed to signify acceptance of these rules by the entrant. Closing date for entries 31st July 1997.

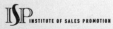

ISP Registration Number: 658
Rules conform to the Institute of Sales Promotion recommended practice.